MW01170771

Glenda
Much Love Always
Your Sister
September
aka
Juanne

Selected
Poems

By

September

POETRY PROSE

LANE

By

September

Self-published
Createspace.com

WWW.Createspace.com

ISBN 978-1440435225

Poetry Prose Lane by September

Copyright 2008 by September

All rights reserved.

Book design cover by September

Available from Amazon.com,
Createspace.com and directly from
the Author by mail: PO Box 1525
Bridgeport CT 06601

Printed in the United State of
America

First Printing October 2008

About this Collection

September has compiled over fifty poems, a few prosaic writings, some light verse, songs, prayers and some short quips for you to ponder and enjoy.

We hope somewhere in this collection, you will find one that is heartfelt for you.

And should anyone have a desire to have the writing of their choice beautifully framed to give as a gift or to keep, feel free to contact the author with your request.

DEDICATION

Dedicated to my Father, who is rich,
God!

I thank him above all others.

ACKNOWLEDGEMENTS

I thank my pastor, Pastor Mary Lee McBride and my church for their support.

I also thank my son, Charles for his contribution, as well as my daughter, Jowanne for her contribution.

My mother, Eula, who has endured more than any one woman I have come to know, endured with grace, love, and faith. God rest her soul.

My God-given sisters, Nancy, Francis, Glenda, Melissa, Tracy, Lucia, Maxine, Shirley, Esther, Flora, Brenda, Donzella and Vicki.

My blood brothers, living and dead, Johnny, Larry, Chester, Wayne, Anthony, Bryan, Kevin, and Travis.

My God-daughters, Sandra, Dianne, and Dawn.

My God-brother, Terrell.

My God-mothers, Addie and
Rosetta.

My God-fathers, Washington and
Pete.

My too-many to name "little ones"
that come to me for bandages and
hugs.

My too-many to name that come to
me for housing and food.

My niece and my friend, Keturah
who has inspired me and motivated
me in ways no one else has. In ways
no one else could. God bless her.

Our family friend G.A. Franchi for
always being there.

And to all my readers, I give thanks
and ask God to continue to bless
and have mercy on each and every
one of YOU

.

POEMS

TO TOUCH A CLOUD

To touch a cloud
And scream so
very loud!

To smell the fresh
air after the rain.
To feel the calm
after the pain.

To catch a cloud
and ride a rainbow
is to live and to
grow.

To hold fire in
your hand and not
get burned.

To walk past love
and not yearn
is to know some
things cannot
be done.

To share your
rainbow is to live
and grow.

Lift your scream,
so very loud.

Lift to touch a
cloud.

INSTEAD

Sometimes I wish
I could be an artist

And paint my
cares away

Instead of trying
desperately to put

them in the words
I say.

I wish I could sing
my problems

Till they could be
sung no more

Instead of writing,
writing, over and
over as so often
done before

Or maybe tick-
tock my worries

11

Till the tocks no
longer be ticked

Instead of
composing and
reposing,

So as not to say
this writer is
licked.

But as I continue
with little quirks

I find my words
on paper still
works.

I CARE ABOUT ME!

So, You
Think I
don't care
about me
Well, I Care
More Than
You Know

Simply
Because I
Care So
Much For
You

Doesn't
Mean I
Can't Close
The Door

The Door
That I Leave

Open To
Hurt & Pain

The Door
That Leads
To Your
Personal
Gain

I Can Close
it, Tho,
Hard It May
Be- For

It Is Heavy
And Much
Larger Than
Me

But I Can
Receive
Strength
From Within

More Than
Enough To
Shut Out The
Wind

So You Think
I Don't Care
About Me.

Well, I Care
- I Do - More
Than You
Know

I Care. You
Shall See. I
Care About
Me.

<u>FOR YOU</u>

For you, my love,
I would do most
anything

For you, my love,
total love I could
bring

You are my
sunshine, no
matter what the
day

You are my
happiness in so
many ways.

So much joy I
have yet to receive

So much, I have
yet to give

Monetary things
mean so little to
us.

Spiritual feelings
we seek with a
lust.

It provides us with
a deeper view of
what we have and
shows us what to
come

We have only to
be patient to see
our rising sun.

If you give me the
time to show my
love, our love will
be that of a love
story—

Happiness from
start to end.

I AM AS I WAS

Could it be
possible that what
I seem to believe
from your
suggestions are
mistakenly
interpreted
Thereby causing
erroneous
assumptions on
my part
That can not truly
be corrected?

And if these
assumptions are
somehow altered
to reveal the for-
realness within,
isn't it possible
That the initial
mistake will be
repeated?

"They" say we
learn from our
mistakes, and one
does not make the
same mistake
twice, is it not
factual that history
repeats itself?

Regardless of the
new form, shape,
that one
particular item
obtains, results
and response
to similar
situations are
basically
instinctive.
Then does ones'
instinct protect
him or
reverse?

Incidentally,
through all of
life's challenges, I
am as I was.

There Are Times

There are times in
one's life it seems
as if no one really
cares.

The bills are over
the income and
the cupboards are
bare.

Sex is infrequent
and there is a lack
of fun.

Too much rain
going on and not
enough sun.

But we keep on
striving to reach
that higher status

To pay bills that
keep staring at us

To feed the little
ones that can't
feed themselves
And to clothes
their little butts
with more than
bells.

We get depressed
and go out for a
few drinks.

And for a short
time, completely
drunk, we can
think!

Then we sober
and dance our
cares away

Along with
everything we
thought we could
say.

There are times in
life when it seems
no one cares.

No one believes in
us or has any time
to share our hopes
and aspirations of
easier times to
come.

They nod their
heads while their
mouths say ho-
hum!

WHAT DO YOU DO?

Once in a while
you meet some
one that you
feel you want
to know
forever!

Then that
person, in
return, shows
you that they
want to know
you forever!

What do you
do?
Lots a things.
You smile
together. You
cry together.
You run against
all

pain and you
find yourselves
singing in the
rain.

You cry
together. You
sing in the rain
and run, run
very hard
against all the
pain.

Once in a while
you meet some
one that knows
you better than
you know
yourself.

They think like
you, they
respond and re-

act the same as
you do.
They tell
stories,
paint pictures,
and draw the
same crowds,
just like you.

What do you
do?

You lean on
each other.
You travel back
in time and
wish you had
met them so
much
earlier in your
life.
You daydream
a lot.

You miss them.
You love them.
And, for once
in your life,
they love you.
They miss you.
They tell you
so.
Then ......
Life can be so
wonderful. For
once in your
life, you truly
want to live.

Then that
person dies.

And inside, so
do you.

Even still, you
smile together.

You cry
together. You
sing in the rain
and run, run
very hard
against all the
pain.

For Your 24th Birthday!

You shall have 24 candles on a 24 layered cake

With 24 quests and their 24 mates

You will have 24 drinks and play 24 songs

Dance 24 dances and right 24 wrongs!

HAPPY BIRTHDAY 24 YEAR OLD!

guy- dude

Thursday, I met
this guy who dug
me

Saturday, I go see
this guy who digs
me

Sunday I lay
quietly.

These dudes come
and they go

Some of them
have been here
before

Some of them are
new

And some of them
are nevermore.

  The cycle
continues, until

when I meet that
ONE
who comes again,
and again and
finally,
again!

MYSTIC MAN

There was no love
involved. It just
happened to
evolve.

There was nothing
from the heart.
We knew it from
the start.

He came -
granted- from
nowhere

He spoke softly
and distinctive

Materializing
from thin air

His being, my
incentive

So easily he
became a part of
us

Our house, now a
home reborn

His sincerity
inspired my trust.

The Comings of Spring

The comings of
Spring often
brings laughter
and gaiety to the
heart

The comings of
Spring often
allows gay bright
expressions from
the dark

The comings of
Spring introduces
children playing,
flowers blooming,
pouring rains, and
fruit juices.

The comings of
Spring shouts of
love and romantic
feelings

The comings of
Spring sprouts
festive get-
togethers under all
ceilings

The comings of
Spring are
joyously received
Greatly
anticipated and
warmly accepted

The comings of
Spring are
ceremoniously
conceived
Heartily
welcomed, leaving
winter rejected.

Spring is here, the
birds sing

The crickets chirp
and chores are
done

Songs are written
just for Spring -

They are sung just
for fun.

The comings of
Spring touches
everyone.

FROM:
TRUCKSTOPS

Every damn day I
wonder when are
you gonna come
home

And every single
day I question why
you have to be
gone so long.

I miss you terribly,
and vibrators take
the physical need
away

But they don't do a
damn thing for
that "ole"
closeness of you
crave.

I love you more
than you'll ever
know

You always and
always continue
my hearts' glow

I want you more
than anyone has
ever wanted
anyone.

I'm hooked on you
and I can't let go.

Please love me
too.

Don't let me be
just a stop on the
way

Let me be a
thought lingering
day by day

Let me be "home"
when the road
turns in

37

Let me be "return"
when the road
turns again

If I can't be, then,

For God's sake,

Leave me. . . . .

ALONE!

IRREPARABLE

Seems to me
you've been away

For a long, long
time.............

And here you are
now, saying

"You're mine all
mine".

How can you
think after all
these years

That I can pick up
after all those
tears

There is no way
we can even be
friends

There is no way
we can do it
again.

So much time has
passed.

The memories
have died.
The feelings have
subsided.

To renew would
not last.

Give Me Love

Looking for
the
materialistic
things, not so
much for me

Outside
appearances
mean so
much, but
inside is more
important to
see.

Never mind
your muscles
and scars

Give me
depth, give
me truth

Something
pure with
strong root

More that
will last

Less that will
pass

Some forever
realness in
this world of
changing
standards

More than
enough to get
me past
tomorrow's
unknowing
candors.

Give me love.

MOMENT OF
MISERY

Moma, I want to
come home.

I'm tired of this
city; tired of being
alone.

So tired of being
sad and depressed

You could call it
homesick, I guess.

Moma, I want to
come home, but I
can't cause. . . . .

Moma, I love you,
I miss you.

God, I feel lost.

These feelings
expressed are true

"Wished I had
never left you."

Once you leave
there is no going
back.

Time and time I
beg for death.

It'll come, just as
sho as I'm black.

It'll pass over and
end my misery.

My loneliness and
grief will fade.

I'll be content, just
wait and see.

My heavy burden
will then be laid.

YOU WONDER

Can there be so
much mystery in
life that all our
thoughts are only
suppositions of
fantasies that
never exist and
surely never will?

Or can life be so
simple that in
order to survive
we ourselves
mystify it and add
to the confusion?

And love, how
bout that love?
Could it be a
fools' paradise
and merely that
and nothing
more?

Still . . .
You wonder.

45

AT THE PARK

Puerto Ricans
from New York

White Folks from
Indiana

Blacks from
Connecticut

Chinese from
Louisiana

And they all
gather at the park

Seldom alone,
seldom at dark

Nationalities
unheard of, some
themselves don't
really know, how
they came or how
they go.

Look alikes that
remind you of
someone else

Unfamiliar faces
that are unfamiliar
to themselves.

And you watch as
they go by

As they run, and
catch frisbees in
the sky.

BOY IN THE HOOD

Little boy in the hood
Come shoot your gun

The girls are getting raped in the streets and on the corner, crack is on the run.

Where's the little boy in the hood to shoot the gun?

He was handcuffed and locked up last night about a quarter to one.

Where's the little boy in the hood to shoot the gun?

Oh, that boy, he
was scholar
shipped to Yale
last month.

He boarded his
train last night
about a quarter to
one.

RE-DONE

There is a time
soon to come
to erase all the
sorrows of a heart
undone.

A time to cleanse
the filth of lies
told and create
new bodies and
new souls

For those that
want and those
that want not

To begin anew
with all they've
got

There is a time
soon to come
for so many
refreshing chores
to be done.

EYE-ON

Black, brown, and
blue eyes

Round one, square
ones

Watching your
thighs

Eyes that laugh
and cry

Eyes that tell
stories

Eyes that lie

EYES on You
and
EYES on ME

REMEMBER THEM?

RE-ELECT
Reagan (or Bush)
TODAY?

Reagan must be
out of his tree
If he thought
cutting welfare
and food stamps
didn't intimidate
me.

He couldn't really
feel that the teeny-
teeny tax cut was
any big deal

Rob from the poor
and give to the
rich

The dirty-crazy
son-of-a-bitch

When he gets his,
I hope its sl-o-o-w
So he can feel
every welfare and
food stamp go.

Bush will learn
the hard way as
most know-it-alls
do.

They ain't gonna
get four by
dividing two into
two.

It will only get
them the number
of re-election
votes due.

WHAT YOU SEE

If you like what
you see

Come on, come
on, and boogie

If you're digging
my looks

baby, I'll show you
how to cook

Said, if you like
what you see and
wanna be with
me,

just be sure you're
free to boogie

If my thighs got
your eyes

And my lips got
your hips

And my tits got
your wits
Just wink a wink
at me

Let me know you
like what you see

Come on-come
on-come on and
boogie

Said, if you're
digging my looks

Oh baby, I'll show
you how to cook

If my beads melt
your freeze

And my smell
swells your tail
And my strut gets
your gut

Don't wanna hear
no buts

Just wanna know
your stuff and if
I like what I see-
I'm gonna boogie

If I like what I
see-You can't stop
me

Boogie - boogie -
boogie - boogie.

LIL BLACK
SKINNY GIRL

Lil Black Skinny
Girl wit nappy
hair

Curious mind,
fairskinned and
troubled heart

Headaches at six
years of age-What
a start!

Lil Black Skinny
Girl wit nappy
hair

Eight brothers, no
sisters, mommie
and dad

Smart as a whip
and twice as sad

Lil Black Skinny

Girl wit nappy
hair

Pretty eyes, lovely
teeth and soft
smile

No guidance - Lil
girl growing wild

And wild she
grows as wild she
knows

and foolish she
does as foolish she
was

and slick she gets
as slick she wets

So wise the wisest
are not sure

So cunning, the
con man is lured

In traps she falls
and does/does not
get caught

Set traps. And
traps set are/are
not her fault

Where is she now?

LIL
BLACK SKINNY
GIRL WITH
STRAIGHT
HAIR!

SAME OLE LOVE
SUNG

There it goes
again same jive,
same line

Have your lady
and woman too

leave me lonely
wit nothin to do

Come when you
please

Restricting me,
sucker got my
keys.

I got in this mess
and I'll get out

Just a matter of
time 'foe my mind
shouts

It can't be your
way nor mine
something has got
to give

New jive. New
Line.

POOR LIL BLACK GIRL

Poor lil black girl
wit a troubled
heart

More than enuf
problems from
finish to start

Poor lil black girl
wit mental
anguish

Indecisive
continuous

Weighing life
against a deep
death wish

Poor lil black girl
wit a troubled
heart

College degree

and searching for
truth
Only to learn she's
become old in her
youth

Poor lil black girl
wit mental
anguish

Owning property
and raising kids

Wishing she
hadn't done what
she did.

Poor lil black girl
wit a troubled
heart

Standing alone
without a man at
her side

Exploring life
without a guide.

Poor lil black girl
wit mental
anguish

Emotional wounds
and mental scars
And still not yet
declaring wars

Poor lil black girl
anguished and sad

Where is she now?

RICH LIL
BLACK WOMAN
DAMN MAD! ! !

Teenage RAGE

You know, I was
sitting on the
school steps

And a young girl
came to me

And asked me
who was I

I looked at her and
I thought aloud

Sixteen-high
school dropout
and jobless

Connoisseur of
drugs-same old
street mess

Don't drink to get
drunk-but drink to
dance

Can hustle and

boogie on any
chance

Sixteen with no
identity.

Sixteen and no
one knows me

Sixteen with no
identity.

Sixteen-I want to
know who is she.

Falling In Love
With You

Lying in bed-
waiting for your
call and you may
not call at all

Listening to your
words-watching
you smile makes
my head spin and
my heart beat wild

Falling head over
heels in love with
you

Falling head over
heels in love with
you

Darling, darling,
you're my dream
come true

Unspoken words

we both
understand
Knowing you're
always close at
hand

Makes me

Fall head over
heels in love with
you

Oh - darling -
you're my dream
come true

On the job-
daydreaming-
hoping to hear my
phone ring

Opening a door-
seeing you there-
what joys you
bring

Kissing my lips-

holding your
hands

Makes my heart
skip--not even in
my plans

Falling head over
heels in love with
you

Darling-darling
you're my dream
come true

What will I do
when I fall down

Lord knows, you'd
better be around

Catch me-pick me
up-start all over
again

Like the rain and
the trees in a
strong wind

I'll fall, fall, fall in
deeper than

I'll fall, fall in love
with you-my man

Affair WARNED-
OVER!

So - this must be
the end.

Why else would I
be leaving?

Why else have you
already gone?

Gee, why did it
take so long ?

A new baby - with
no name

A new lady - with
no shame

Two years of pain
with no hope
or anything to
help cope.

This must be the
end.

I couldn't leave
less it was over
and you couldn't
even then.

But I made you.
Yes, I forced you
away, for it took
some one stronger
than yourself.

And my strength
did as always does

I destroyed mine
and your loves.

So this must be
the end.

And still I hope
it's not.

For you're
nothing-but you're
all I've got.

Or had.

Is this the end?
I'm leaving....

You Know!

Will You Let ME
Go?

PICK-UP

As he stood there
in line

Smoking a smelly
cigar

Waiting
impatiently to
dine

She invited him to
the bar.

He accepted, took
her hand and led
her through the
crowd.

Choose seats
nearest the band;
"Two Martinis",
he ordered aloud.

Crushing his cigar
in the tray

His hands seemed
to tremble amid
And his fingers
got in the way

A relaxing touch,
she did.

Without a word of
warning, he began
to gag and choke

She stood!
Frozenly dis-
charming.

His excuse, "sorry,
I'm broke".

He handed her the
check with a
smile, drank his
martini and said,
"see you around,
sometime, my
dear child".

RETIREMENT

"Especially
prepared for Mel
Vwanski"

It has been an
unique
relationship

Sometimes
zinging,
sometimes happy,
and some bad.

Some thinking
times, angry ones,
and some damn
mad!

No excuses,
unused or unsaid

No abuses . . . .

None to be read.

We give you up to
the retired ones
that have earned
theirs

You leave us with
an underemployed

Underfed and
scared (your
replacement)

But sincerely we
are pleased that
you had the guts

To get up, get out,
as we continue to
sit on our butts

And ifs, and
maybes, or
because . . . .

If you hadn't then
we all wouldn't be
lost....without you
- Mel

STAR-AFAR

I wish I could see
a shining star

Not too close, yet
not too far

And that star
would hold the
answer, the
problem, the
solution, the total

An end for death,
a cure for cancer,
a vaccine for HIV,
a cure for AIDS
and make money
obsolete once and
for all

This star that
would shine so
everyone could see

This star that

would enter into
them, you and me
And shine on and
on, forever and a
day

This star much,
much too far
away.

THOUGHTS ALOUD

You have no idea
how much a
telephone call
from the one you
love can do.

If you are
contemplating a
love affair with
someone else and
your phone rings
and it's him----the
one and only one.

Shit---that
contemplating just
disintegrated.

Cause when my
man calls me from
far away . . . . .

My heart skips,
my ass itches, my
emotions rise, I

wet inside my
thighs and
Oouu-h boy,

Ain't another
mother's son in
this whole world
gonna get any love
from this old girl,
cause I love him.

UNITED?

Together we stand
before this man
And profess our
love to be undying

Let it never be
known or even
thought that our
profession of love
was wanly sought

Let today mark
the beginning of
tomorrow

Today's joy to
overshadow future
sorrow

When we are sad
and feeling
despair

Let today be the
reminder of why
we care

And if at
sometime we
decide that we
can't go on,

Let today, let
today, be forever
gone.

WHETHER

The coolness that
comes with
August showers

Reflects on
summer's torrid
disposition

It washes all the
hatred away and
brings in new love
with old
conditions.

Conditions that
tend to loose their
meaning once new
love grows old

And soon we do
more holding,
than leaning for
old love grown
cold

Then September
rain sprinkles the
coolness again
This time to
confirm the
uselessness of a
fan

So then it is
proper for old love
to end

And the search for
new once again,
begins.

But it necessitates
the warmth of the
sun

As October's chill
begins its' run
The adventure is
not one of fun

But more so
serious for that
right someone!

ONE HELLUVA MAN

One Hell of a man
Yes, you are, yes,
you are

With one forever
fan

Always near,
never far.

One Hell of a man
You are to me

Everything I ever
needed a man to
be

That you are, yes
you are

But I could hope
for less

And not get as
much

And I could dream
about more

Never feel your
tender touch

So, I remain the
same as I was
before you ever
walked out that
door

One forever fan
For that Hell of a
man

Yes, you are, you
are for me

One Hell of a man
Yes, you are, you
are

With one forever
fan

Being forever near

and never, never,
never far.
I love you, I want
you, and I need
what you are

One hell of a man
Please take my
hand

Say you'll never
leave again

My hell of a man
Your Forever Fan.

Do you remember
back in the late
seventies, there
was fear in
America? A
shortage of gas?

In 2008 we have
this fear again, but
this is how it was
back then.

THE PROBLEM
IS. . . .

Getting in the gas
line with an even
plate on an even
day................

Only to be told. . .
. ."No gas in the
month of May".

And, then going
to that great White
Sale at all Macy's
stores...........

To find the only
things white on
sale are Doors!

So, wearily taking
it all home to lay
down your head....

Oops, your son
stuck a pin in your
water bed! ! !

Soaking up water
that seems to be
going nowhere.....

And a sympathetic
friend, that says,
"he's been there? ?

WHY?

For every, every,
ache, there is a
desire, yes, a
desire!

For every kind of
contentment, there
is an acceptance of
the same.

For every burn,
there is a fire, yes,
a fire!

For every serious
thought, there is
the thought of
game.

For what do we
owe-that price that
can not be paid.

And who do we
blame, if not
ourselves

The Almighty
stamps "PAID-IN-
FULL" once we
are laid.

And yet as we
live, subtract not
as we dwell.

For every gift of
giving, we take as
we gave

For every receipt
of receiving, we
give as we accept

For every fulfilled
want, we enjoy to
crave

For every, every,
surge of strength,
we ignore the
depth.

For what do we
know of our needs
un-met
And who can't tell
us the simple is
complex.

For what have we
learned if we
know nothing at
all

And what can we
earn, if we miss
our call?

For every, every
request, there is a
need, yes, a need

For every
opportunity there
is a taker

For every, every
failure, there is an
undone deed

For every chance,
there is a maker.

For what are we if
we don't
participate

And who are you
if you don't
reciprocate?

WHY?

CONTACT

Now, in the
quietness of peace
of mind.
A quiet some
never find.

I long to reach to
touch tenderly the
heart of one
needing to be felt

To inspire into
one pleasurable
tarts of tidbits that
smoothly melt.

Into a man I
desire to bring the
sweetness of
Winters Spring

I yearn to warm
his body all over
and relax all his
tensions away

To be for him a
four-leaf clover
encouraging good
fortune to stay

So, now, I indeed,
inspire into
someone
pleasurable tarts
of tidbits that
smoothly melt

I reach, and
indeed, I am
touching tenderly
the heart of one
needing to be felt.

All in the
quietness of peace
of mind.
A quiet some
never find.

A DEFINITE
PART OF ME

And you'll always
be

A definite part of
me

You draw me
pictures of things
I've never seen

You paint
portraits of places
I've never
dreamed.

You dance me
with real meaning
You stand strong
when I'm weak
leaning

And you'll always
be

A definite part of
me
You do things for
me that no one
else can

You make me
proud that you're
my man

And you'll always
be

A definite part of
me.

Tributes
To
God

Assurance
Prayer

And I pray,

God, make a way.

And I know

He has already
done so.

And I pray.

God, see me
through.

I pray for me and
you.

Prayer for Presence

Dear God
Let us be aware of
your presence in
our lives at all
times, so that our
words, our
thoughts, and our
actions are all
subject to your
will.

                Amen

GLO-RI-OUS

I'm gonna write a
pra-aise so glo-ri-
ous

That it out shines
any ot-ther

I'm gonna sing a
pra-aise so glo-ri-
ous

That it out rings
any ot-ther

Glo-ri-ous, glo-ri-
ous, is the Lord!

Glo-ri-ous, glo-ri-
ous, is the Lord!

He has done more
for me

Than any man can
see

He has been there
in my time of need

And when I was
doing well, his
test I would not
fail.

He kept me. Took
me from wrong.

I'm gonna sing
this pra-aise - so
glo-ri-ous

That out rings any
o-ther

I'm gonna sing,
glo-ri-ous, glo-ri-
ous is the Lord!

For now - and -
always

I'm gonna sing,
glo-ri-ous, glo-ri-
ous is the Lord!

For now - and –
always

A SONG FOR GOD

I want to come in
now - Lord

I want to come
home tonight

Cause you, God,
can make
everything alright

I did not say one-
thing, Lord.

I did not say some
things, Lord

I said "only you,
God" can make
everything alright.

It's raining out
here.

I want to come in.
I am cold, Lord.

I want to come
home now, Lord.
I want to come
tonight.

I want to Thank
You God for
making everything
al-right.
I want to Thank
you, Lord, for
letting me in
tonight.

Ay-I I am warm,
Lord.
Ay-I I am home,
Lord.

Ay-I I'd been out
in the cold for so
long, Lord.

I'm glad to be
home.

Ay-I I'd been out
in the cold for so
long, Lord.
I'm glad to be in.
Ay-I I am warm
God in your
embrace

Lord help me keep
my faith. Don't let
me go back in the
cold.

Keep my faith.

It's warm, Lord. I
want to stay. It's
so warm, Lord. I
want to stay.

(in a speaking
voice-a call for
sheep)

All those that feel
the need to come
in, now is the
time. Step

forward and let
God embrace you
and strengthen
your faith. Come
in now, out from
the cold. God can
make everything
all right, he
already has, come
in now, come
home and say
Thank You, God
and feel the
warmth of coming
in.

[Return to Song]

Ay-I I'm so glad,
Lord. You let me
in.

Ay-I I'm so glad,
Lord. That you're
my friend.

A PRAYER

Lord
Give ME...........

Strength to
withstand my
battles so that
justice in your
name prevails

Understanding to
deal with my
children in a
righteous way.

A blessed heart to
encourage all to
your ship when it
sails

Courage to go
after that which
comes with each
day.

Motivation to
accomplish the

things I set out to
do.

Wisdom to realize
that I can and
some times can
not.

Equipment
necessary to
achieve the best
for you.

Do not let me
stray in my desires
to please, fulfill,
and withstand

Lest, you let me
die .....
              a
disappointed
woman.

THOSE WHO ARE
SAVED

"Wait on Jesus" was being sung dramatically. The organist kept his rhythm as the drummer gradually increased the momentum. The saxophone notes were timed accurately and distinctively as to send an electric current into the audience every now and then.

It was on one of the saxophone notes, that the organist became influential with his rhythm. Skillfully, his fingers seemingly leaped across the keys. The drummer intensified his tempo and suddenly she jumped from her seat!

She began to dance, the spirit of God within her. Round and round she danced. Her arms lifted high on an angle to form the sign of a V above her head. Faster and faster she went as the drummer roll increased in speed. As she spun in sky blue dress, she became a blur of blue. Round and round she went.

The
ushers formed a
circle around her,
for she danced
with her eyes
closed. Lifting her
feet slightly
higher than the
floor, stepping in
time with the
music.
Kicking
her shoes off
while whirling
blindly, she fell
into the arms
encircling her.
She diverted, only
to fall into more
arms. Round and
round she danced.
Her
breath becoming
ragged, her arms
flying in all
directions! She
spun on. The
organist, the

drummer, the saxophonist, now strengthened with the tambourines encouraged her on.

Round and round she danced, whirling faster and suddenly, just as suddenly as she jumped from her seat............

She stood still!

I THANK YOU
GOD

I Thank You God
for those that can
not thank you for
themselves.

I Thank You
God for my life,
health and
strength.

I Thank You for
my children's life,
health and
strength.

I Thank You for
our soundness of
mind.

I pray you direct
my steps so that I
may be guided to
live my life as you
would have me
live my life,

according to your
will and not mine.

I pray that you
help us to teach
and raise the
children, all
children, as you
would have them
taught and raised.

I pray that you
give me the
compassion to
deal with others
and understanding
as you would have
me to understand.

I Thank You for
loving me and for
instilling in my
heart love for you.

I Thank You for
your blessings and
mercy and pray
you continue your

blessings and
mercy in my
present and future
as you have done
in my past.

I Thank You God
for my struggles,
my burdens, my
sickness and my
pain.

I Thank You God
for my joy, my
tears, my love and
my years.

I Thank You God
for those that
neglect to thank
you and for those
that don't know to
thank you.

I Thank You God
for my everything.

GOD SMILES ON ME

Lately, God's been
smiling on me!

Did you hear me?

Lately, God's been
smiling on me.
The sweetest smile
one could ever
see.

That smile, just
for me.

Lately, God's been
smiling on me!

SONGS,
QUIPS,
PROSE
AND
HAIKUS

SONGS

IT'S ALL RIGHT

I've
been down for so
long - It hasn't
always been this
way
What
debt must I pay -
How long before
I'm able to say
It's a-
l-l r-i-g-h-t again
It's a-l-l r-i-g-h-t
again
This
a-l-l w-r-o-n-g
doesn't seem to
end
What
did I ever do to
come this far
down
I've
been down for so
long

What
did I ever do so
wrong
          Seems
like I owe for so
many mo'e
          Than
myself
          I'm
down, so very
down-low -very
down to the
ground
          What
debt must I pay –

How long before
I'm able to say
          It's a-
l-l r-i-g-h-t again
It's a-l-l r-i-g-h-t
again
          This
a-l-l wrong
doesn't seem to
end
          But I
know - one day

It's all gonna blow
away
                One
day very soon, I'll
say
                "It's
a-l-l r-i-g-h-t
again

It's a-l-l r-i-g-h-t
again"

Forever Or Never

I have to be with
you forever or
never

There's too much
love between us
To part would
only break our
hearts

When you're near
me-I'm near you
So much so - you
turn me away

And Turn I do -

Then you reach
for me to stay

You have to be
with me forever or
never

You're the only
man I can fight

with, break up and
never leave

(mans part)

You're the only
lady I can hold
onto without
pressures or
cleaves

I have to be with
you forever or
never

It's too late to say
never - now

Forever and
Always -
somehow

I have to be with
you-my love

Can't stand the
pain of knowing I

won't see you
again
Can't deal with
the thought

That we won't
make up after
we've fought

Can't handle the
pressures of going
through life
without you

Knowing Our
Love is a Love
Story True

I have to be with
you forever-or
never

It's too late to say
never - now

Forever and
Always -
somehow

I have to be with
you forever - now.

QUIPS

Deceptive
Perception

We deceive
ourselves, to
relieve others . . . .
. . . why?

****

Can Do

I can write a love
story, or an eternal
poem, a famous
quote, a
devastating book
for all.

****

ON FAITH

　　　　We live
to be screened,
　　　　Tested,
and selected,

                    By
God; for Heaven
or Hell.
                    We
fly. But fail, we
die.

****

White

With all that this
dear earth has to
give, why are they
selfish, making it
hell to live?

****

On Yesterday

Yesterday, my
heart yearns for a
year of yesterdays!

****

PROSE

ready?

every so often I
find I'm up
against the wall

push myself back
and I fall.

stand up to be
knocked down
agin

I keep on trying, I
gotta win.

look out! I've
managed to move
one inch.
cry, cry, cry, I'm
farther away than
befo'

give a go agin,

shit!

someone closed de
doe
so what! I've
found the key

but, I'll be...

some fool one else
changed the damn
lock.

gotta give it one
mo' go, I ain't
through

hitting hard,
gonna break this
circle
can't let it break
me, gonna break
you.

try my patience
and you will see

you go mad before
me.

I've got a will that
says try it till

I can't try no
more..............

kill me or

OPEN UP THAT
DOOR.

****

ON BEING
BLACK

To get through life
being black is like
getting through a

love affair

without getting
hurt.

only those with
will....... Will.

To come up out
of the ghetto on an
equal = level with
those that "got
over"

Is to come UP
as an ABOVE
average 'nigger'..
but....

you're NOT!

HE WAS HIM

I sit on my psych
couch

And I rock and I
rock

And I stop crying,
and my nose
doesn't run
anymore,

But I hurt the
same.

And I wonder why
did I love him.

And who was he
anyway

And why it's not
happening the
same as before

Did it have to hurt

so deep and for so
long.
Will it ever end?

Will I live again?

Or will I crack on
my psych couch?

I pray for relief
anyway it comes

Or maybe I'll
gather enuf
strength to kill
myself and...

FUCK praying-it's
not working

UNTITLED(S)

We seem to know
where we're going

How we are gonna
get there

We seem not to
know when or
why

But still, we are
going. . . .

Past all obstacles,
through all

truths and lies, we
wander

continuously.
Destination
Foretold!

I want to write a
book. A book to be
read

A poem. A poem
to be felt

I want to write a
story. So little
ones may enjoy

I want to write a
song, so all may
sing.

I want to write, so
YOU may read.

Students -
Teachers that
don't teach: only
speak

Students that don't
learn: only yearn
Teachers -
Students that
would, really
would, do better.

PAIN-PAIN-PAIN

Sometimes when
words are not
sufficient to ease
a pain of words
spoken, we know
THAT pain is not
physical and is
deeper than the
mind - not
insulted

HEART BORN

When words are
not *necessary* to
relieve a pain of
words spoken . . .
SILENT
ACCEPTED
APOLOGY

HIGH DEFINED

Such a peaceful
wonderful night

Such a quiet
enjoyable evening,
like a new feeling
– un-worded -
found.

The feeling of
optisience - where
one
*emergessmoothlyintoth
eatomosphere,*

one's entire
existence is
reconstructed to
blendwithforever, to
become a part of
that never ending,
that always; has
been.

That which is and
shall be, God's
pressure,

barometric
pressure, high
blood pressure,

God's pressure.
To suggest we
blend, not bend.
That we ease, not
cease.

That we love - to
develop peace, not
peace alone.

IT will never be –

We must love!

SECTION FROM
A SCHIZO

Another beautiful
summer evening
is drawing near its
end. Another day
he sits and waits,
anticipating a
word from her.
Another day
waiting in vain.
So many of those
days have passed,
he has lost count.
Who is he, who is
she?

Roadrunner would
be most apropos
for her and for him-
Delta Dawn. Both
waiting in the
wrong.

How dare she be
so inconsiderate,
that she don't even

144

phone. What
makes you think
I'm going to die--
not me; some
think of death as a
person, like God
and satan, but
death is a state of
being. One allows
himself to enter
into death.
God needs no
more competition-
satan is plenty
enuff and we
choose to say
death is
competing with
him also?

Death Wish

Soon, very soon
the mind shall
cease to be and
soon, the
breathing will stop
and the blood will
run out and death
will enter the
vagina, and the
body will convulse
and the eyes will
become fixed and
dilated. But the
heart will continue
to beat and beat
and beat till it is
crushed by human
hands. And then
there will be
peace.

When the first
symptoms
appeared, they
rushed her to
Newtown. The

admitting
attendant called
for an emergency
psychotic exam.
She was examined
and placed in an
observation room.
After being there
for fifteen
minutes, the
registering needles
attached to her
vital parts-showed
no signs of life. A
doctor was called
in just as the
convulsions
began, so he tried
a hypodermic to
stop them, and she
began to bleed
profusely, and the
tourniquet didn't
help, and she
continued to
bleed.

With no other
signs of life. The
doctor gave up.
But the heart
continued to
beat, long after the
blood was all
gone, the heart
continued to beat
and beat and then
HE crushed it with
his bare hands.

Her lips formed a
smile on her face,
in the coffin, three
days later, many,
many miles away.

HAIKUS

Leaves

Orange leaves
falling down

They fall fast
without a sound

Changing orange
to brown

Husband

Turning fifty six

I can see the man
for me

And our wedding
fee.

**Children's
Contributions**

From my Son:
Chuck

HAIKU

There is
nothing to play

Nothing
to do

Because
everybody is at
school.

More from Chuck:

Jack Be Be Bop

Jack be Be Bop,
Jack be slick

Jack did the break
dance with a split

He did the
windmill, he did
the spin

Jack did an encore
for Mother Hen

He did the pop, he
did the slide

When everybody
came to see

Jack went to hide

May 17, 1984
Twelve years old

Cultures Are Different

We should
definitely listen
to the many
different things
that we can learn
like who are you,
what you are,
and why you are.
Why you turned
out to be the way
you are.
We must respect
diversity or yes,
there will be a
conspiracy which
is exactly what we
don't want...

So please let us
try to make it
stop!
    By: Jowanne
Charisse Burks
    01-02-96

More from
Jowanne:

Puppies & Babies

Puppies and
babies are the
adorable things in
life.

Babies make you
wake up in the
middle of the
night.

While puppies
make you work in
the middle of the
day.

Leaving nice nasty
messes along the
way.

Puppies and
babies, both
special in their
own style, even

though they both
are very wild.

April 20, 1995

**SPECIAL POEM
DEDICATION**

**TO MY
MOTHER**

MOTHER

You must have
given me lots a
love

Mother
You must have
given me lots a
hugs

For all through
my life as no man
loved me. I felt
LOVED, very
LOVED!
It must have come
from thee.

You must have
given me a
foundation of trust
You must have
given me the
patience of Job

Mother

For the things that
I could not discuss
I knew how to out
wait my woes

Mother

You must have
known in advance
what I would need

Mother

You must have
known how many
I would lead

For you gave me
an abundance of a
lot of stuff to take
me and many
others past the
rough times and
hard times. And
you must have
listened to all I
had to say.

You must have
taught me how to
really pray.
And of course you
were there
whenever I shed a
tear

There always to
shy away my every
fear

Mother

You must have
comforted me
when I was sad

Mother

You must have
shared my joy
when I was glad

But when I think
back on how much

you've done for
me

And how much
you've always
been there,
I remember how
much I have never
heard you laugh.

Oh, I've seen you
smile the prettiest
smile this whole
world wide

I've seen you eyes
twinkle and gleam

One of the
loveliest sights
I've ever seen.

But, I've never
heard you laugh.

You have
chuckled at some
of my jokes.

And looked rather
comical as I
practiced my
dance strokes
But, I've never
heard you laugh.

I realize what all
you have gone
through and how
much you
continue to endure

I pray for
"laughter" from
you, Mother, so I
can know for once
your happiness
was sure.

Mother- For all
that you have done
for me and given
me

I have only this
poem to dedicate
in return to thee

And I'm sure I
speak for Johnny,
Larry, Chester,
Wayne, Anthony,
Bryan, Kevin, and
Travis.

For we have loved
you and treasure
your laughter.

AUTHORS
COMMENTS

Why does one write poetry, prose, short stories and descriptive paragraphs?

Why? To express their emotions, their confusion, their thoughts and desires.

For interested persons only:

Poetry Prose Lane attempts to express a number of things.

I've often had to review a poem in a creative writing class and felt that the author as interpreted by the teacher and the students could be wrong.

The author offers the following explanations of selected prose if any person decides to use them in a writing course.

It is wonderful to have an explanation behind poetry, but you and I know that it would be much too lengthy to put here.

Therefore in the interest of keeping things short and sweet I've given my interpretation of the following 3 selected prose pieces:

1. THOSE WHO ARE SAVED: A descriptive paragraph using a simile and some alliteration to show the beauty of one receiving the Holy Spirit.

(Note) Educators should look for students' ability to determine the descriptions, alliterations and similes.

2. DEATH WISH: Depression is shown in this short piece of prose. The person displayed wanted so badly to face death after being raped that she played out the

entire scene in her mind and was only relived and
happy after she had been buried which suggests even
in death there is life.

3. SECTION FROM A SCHIZO: This prose piece
depicts a lonely man who switches his concentration
from the fact that the woman in his life has again
caused him grave disappointment to thoughts of death
that involves a theory on the "God vs. Satan"
challenge.

FOR EDUCATORS ONLY

I've devised a game for selected poetry pieces that will assist with the reading of these poems. I chose the letter "S" to describe the poems listed below.

Your job as the teacher is to have your students give their impressions and reasons as to why I chose the words that I chose and then have them chose another word to describe the same poem.

They can only use one word descriptions. You may limit them to any letter of your choice that their word must start with. Or you may limit them to the letter "S" as I limited myself.

I chose 'S' because a lot of words that started with "S" actually describe the different readings that you have just enjoyed and pondered.

Ask your students why they think I chose that word. Ask them what word would they have chosen and ask them why to start conversation about the poem.

Following are my choices:

1. Savvy for I AM AS I WAS
2. Sincere for I CARE ABOUT ME
3. Sexy for WHAT YOU SEE
4. Selective for PICK-UP
5. Sensible for UNITED?
6. Successful for POOR LIL BLACK GIRL

7. Sassy for LIL BLACK SKINNY GIRL
8. Sophisticated for WHY?
9. Spectacular for TO TOUCH A CLOUD
10. Spellbinding for CONTACT
11. Sociable for THE COMINGS OF SPRING

There should be no wrong answers as long as a reasonable explanation is given for their choice of word(s).

Keep it fun!